FRAGMENTS OF CERULEAN

NEAL H. PARIS

Revelation House Works

DEDICATION

This is for the broken, the unseen, and the forgotten.

I see you.

I remember you.

And you are not broken.

"There's no time. Takes what's yours. Leave what isn't. Good day."

—The Redbird

Author's Note

These pieces came unexpectedly when I stopped trying to explain myself and started listening instead.

This collection isn't linear. It doesn't offer resolution. But it understands what it means to carry trauma and grief in silence. If you find yourself somewhere inside these pages, I hope you feel a little less alone—and a little more real.

— Neal H. Paris

P. S. When words aren't enough, turn to the last page for the music that fueled the madness.

CONTENTS

PHASE ONE:
SHATTER

This is the destabilization.

The first time the mirror twitches.

You are no longer the narrator of your own life.

Grief

there's no shape or color to define grief

silent screams and unseen pain drown out any signs of life

it stitches our memories together with a rusty dull needle

leaving behind a life infected with sorrow and shame

for things that we were too young to name

Forgotten Highway

My hands are steady on the wheel as I drive down an unfamiliar road. There's a sign up ahead, caught in the headlights.

It looks like a traffic sign—but not one I've seen before. When it comes into focus, it's not what I expected.

It's hand-painted.

Crooked.

TURN BACK BEFORE YOU REMEMBER

Foot on the brake, my hands start to tremble.

Cold sweat beads along my brow.

What's happening to me?

I shake my head—a weak attempt to snap back into something I can recognize. It doesn't work.

This doesn't feel like my body. Doesn't feel like my mind.

The need to get as far away from that sign as possible overtakes me. Something pulls me forward.

Urgent.

Invisible.

I hit the gas. Yellow lines blur beneath my tires—quick, repetitive, counting down for a moment I'm not ready to face.

My body starts to feel weightless.

Unreal.

I can't keep going.

This road...

this feeling—

Something's wrong.

Brakes screech to a halt as blurred trees sharpen into focus.

Everything is too still.

Too quiet.

Jagged shards of air fill my lungs.

Buzzing rips through my skull. Every thought shatters.

White-hot light bursts behind my eyes.

A voice.

Soft.

Calling my name.

We're laughing.

Running.

A beach.

I reach out—her small hand in mine.

Then—

It's gone.

The sun is gone.

The joy is gone.

I'm alone, holding a tiny jacket.

SCREAMING

SCREAMING her name.

THE LOST NAME

Everyone in my life is suddenly calling me by the wrong name.

Not a nickname.

Not a mispronunciation. A completely different name— spoken with absolute certainty, like it's always been mine.

I correct them.

They laugh.

I check my ID. My mail. Even my birth certificate.

They've all changed too.

As I search for something—anything—that proves I'm not crazy, the living room floor disappears beneath a sea of paperwork.

Exhausted by the weight of my failed mission, I sit in the middle of it, surrounded by evidence that only proves their version of me.

I know who I am. I just need to prove it.

Maybe... maybe the account.

The remote feels slippery in my hands as I fumble with it, trying to find the button for my streaming service.

I click on my profile, hoping for relief, for confirmation. But all of the thumbnails have changed.

The room starts to spin, and reality doesn't feel tangible anymore.

Every movie, every show… replaced by photos of me.

And beside each one: the name they keep calling me.

I scroll. And scroll. And scroll.

My photo.

My photo.

My photo.

My photo.

And *that* name.

Memories On Trial

I've served on jury duty before, but this is the first time I've heard of the defendant being a memory.

No opening statements.

No lawyers.

Just a screen, a dozen strangers, and a question: True, False, or Altered?

Figures move across the screen—hazy shapes, soft around the edges.

The colors are vivid, unnaturally bright.

The words are clear.

A larger person is speaking to a smaller one. Their conversation is sharp, heated—centered around betrayal, regret.

The man is angry.

The woman is silent.

He says she's worthless. That he wishes he'd never met her.

The view is low—like a camera placed on the ground and tilted upward. It isn't shown from either of their perspectives. It feels like the observer is hiding. Peering around a corner.

Strange...

***

Back in the jury room, we quietly follow protocol and take a blind vote before discussion:

3 false.

9 true.

0 altered.

Juror 1 suggests we watch it again.

We file back into the courtroom.

This time, something stirs in my chest as we watch.

That voice—it sounds familiar.

By the end of it, I'm almost certain:

This memory might be *mine*.

Why would they assign me to this case if it's mine?

***

We've been deliberating for hours.

Some jurors are growing restless.

Irritated.

One of them slams his hand on the table.

"Why in the hell would anyone think this is false?" he snaps.

"People fight like this all of the time. You all are crazy if you don't think this is real."

After a few jurors murmur their agreement with him, I speak.

"Whose memory is this?"

Silence.

"Why does it matter if it's true or false?" I press.

"Don't you think the angle is strange? The haze? The distance?"

The angry one throws up his hands in exasperation.

"That's not what we're here to decide!"

I meet his gaze. "But it matters."

The room goes quiet. Each juror exchanging uncomfortable glances with each other.

I look at each one of them—daring them to tell me why I'm wrong.

A lady who's been quiet until now speaks up. "Well, she might have a point.", she says reluctantly, shifting her gaze toward the angry guy.

"There are some unusual characteristics displayed in the memory we watched." another juror chimes in, while pushing his glasses up.

A few more nod. Others add their agreement.

Angry guy sits quietly, fuming, but doesn't argue with us as we talk through it.

"Let's take another vote." the foreman suggests.

This time, the results are unanimous.

***

We're summoned back into the courtroom and moodily shuffle our way to our seats.

The judge asks for our decision.

Our jury foreman grunts and stands to deliver it: "We, the jury, find this memory to be false."

The judge nods. "Very good," she says. Then adds with a wave to the back of the courtroom, "Bring her in."

A small girl—maybe six years old—is escorted in by a stern woman in a blue suit.

The judge speaks gently, directly to the child.

"Your memory has been deemed false. This wasn't your fault, and this message isn't yours to carry."

"In cases like yours, we find it necessary to erase false memories—

because the weight you carry will determine your future in ways you can't understand yet."

"You can forget now, if you're ready to be at peace."

"That is the court's decision."

The gavel bangs.

PHASE TWO:
DESCENT

You fall inward.

The world no longer makes sense.

You don't get out—

you go deeper.

Broken Clock

I run from wall to wall, frantically tracing my hands along each one—trying to feel for a hidden opening. I'm trapped.

How did I get here?

How do I get out?

I turn to face the wall I just checked.

Wait.

That door wasn't there before.

The wood is cracked and splintered in places. It feels ancient, like it knows something I don't.

I reach for the handle with caution, like it's an unpredictable beast that needs to be tamed—my hand grabs nothing but air. A lock appears in its place.

A lock?

I don't have a key. I don't have anything—just myself, and four walls.

Such a simple, impossible little thing between me and freedom.

Leaning in, I notice something etched into the metal. The language is unfamiliar, but somehow, I understand it.

I flinch. *How do I understand it?*

Unsettled, I ignore the question and read it again.

FREE YOURSELF. YOU HAVE THE KEY.

Not helpful. Of course a riddle shows up to taunt me.

I pat my pockets anyway, just in case.

Nothing.

Why am I here? I didn't choose this.

The injustice of it all sends fire through my bones. Rage boils up and takes over. I scream, kick, punch the door until my fists go numb.

"LET ME OUT! Somebody—anybody—LET ME OUT!"

My voice echoes off the walls like it's never going to land anywhere.

It's no use.

My arms ache. My head throbs. My body feels hollow. I blink back unwelcome tears.

Anger drains from me as I collapse, and slide down the door, landing hard on the floor.

No one's coming.

A soft sound above me.

Click

***

I'm still on my hands and knees when the door creaks open. I don't wait for permission—I push myself up and lunge through the opening into a room filled with clocks.

They cover every wall floor to ceiling. Each one different. Unique.

Directly in front of me, there's an old antique clock shaped like a birdhouse, and a small red bird perched outside it, waiting to announce the time.

Every clock has a face, but none of the hands match. They're all pointing to different moments, frozen mid-tick.

One clock draws my eye. It looks so ordinary—like something I've seen a thousand times in other places.

It's cracked. The face is shattered. It's not pristine like the others, and I can't stop staring at it. It's so ordinary and broken, but it's my favorite. My cheeks go hot at the thought. Impulsively, I reach up to take it off the wall.

It doesn't belong here.

It belongs with me.

Something shifts in the air as I reach for my clock, and the little red bird catches my attention. Tiny screws that hold its delicate beak start to whirr, and it begins to speak.

In a voice so devastatingly soft and familiar, like a quiet song, as it says:

"There's no time. Take what's yours. Leave what isn't. Good day."

A pulse fills the atmosphere.
The broken clock comes off the wall easily now. Its cracked face glows faintly. Currents warm my grasp as I clutch the clock tightly to my chest.

I turn toward the door I came through—

It's gone.

***

A long, narrow hallway looms before me. One light flickering at the far end. Unpredictability is almost comforting now.

Have I been here before?

My blood is rushing through my ears and panic is lodged in my throat.

Even though there's only one way forward, I'm afraid I'll get lost. I try to name why—fear of taking the wrong turn, fear of wandering alone forever, fear of never reaching the light. Trying to understand it seems useless.

My thoughts scream at me, but my logic has no room in a place like this. It's not wanted. Not welcomed.

My feet, although unsteady, begin to move before I need to tell them to. We're moving toward the light.
There's only one path. Stop being so afraid.

Fear and uncertainty grip my soul, but I keep moving anyway.

The light pulses gently ahead. A heartbeat waiting at the end of the world.

My steps echo louder than they should. Each one sounds like it's being recorded—archived.

When I reach the light, it isn't a bulb or a window.

It's a doorway, and beyond it—just mist.

No walls. No ground. Just a soft, glowing fog that hums when I breathe near it.

I stumble. Unsure.

Then, the clock in my arms ticks. The hands move.

Only once.

The shattered face cracks a little more, and inside it I see something strange:

a reflection of myself—not as I am, but as I became—the version of me that chose to stay lost. Trapped.

I'd rather be free in the fog than trapped in this unforgiving hallway.

There's no hesitation. I run toward the unknown.

VACANCY

2am flashes on the dial—it won't let me forget how long I've been driving or how sleep deprived I am—betrayal by AM/FM radio.

I roll my eyes at myself, but a neon sign up ahead interrupts my self admonishment.

VAC NCY —flashing proud and broken.

***

Bored and unimpressed with life, the clerk checks me in and tosses me a key. **ROOM 107** is handwritten on the tag.

"Good luck," he says.

...Or maybe he said good night?

He gestures vaguely in the direction to my room and goes back to ignoring me.

So helpful.

***

Worn wallpaper with zig-zag patterns lines the corridor. The carpet is faded and ripe with the smell of mildew, but I'm too tired to care.

How long I have been walking?

I'm almost certain I've passed by the same painting three times, but each time the expression on the face is a little different. The eyes in a different position. The mouth closed in one and open in another.

It must be part of a series.

I stop on the fourth pass to study it. It's the same subject but this time the face looks like a warning. The air is still, but not quiet. An uneasiness settles over me. Like I'm not supposed to be here.

Right. Best not to linger with the haunted art.

I shudder at my poorly timed joke and keep moving.

***

Finally—ROOM 107.

The door swings open while I'm fumbling with key.

Did I forget unlocking it?

Slightly unnerved, I step inside. A mirror stands tall in the center of the room. Upright. Untouched. At first glance, it looks normal. But the longer I stare, the more wrong it feels.

The frame is too clean.

The glass is too clear.

The room reflects behind me, but I'm missing.

No matter how I move, or shift, or lean—

nothing.

I don't know why I reach for it. I just want to know if it's real. If it's actually there.

The glass ripples like water—soft and slow, as I press my hand through the mirror.

It doesn't hurt.

There's no resistance.

Just emptiness.

I'm still watching—my hand vanishing into the mirror—

when something taps my shoulder.

There's no one behind me.

No reflection.

Afraid to move, I look down—with just my eyes to see a hand...

My hand—

resting on my shoulder.

And this, ladies and gentlemen, is how I die.

I yank my hand out of the mirror. The other hand disappears the moment I break contact with it.

I back out of the room.

Fast.

***

I crash through the room across the hall—leaning heavily against the door.

Blinking, I look around.

The air feels quieter in this room, and I'm a little less shaken now.

There's nothing in here but a small glass vial, uncapped, sitting in the center of the floor.

I crouch beside it and pick it up to get a closer look.

The liquid inside is a sharp, unnatural purple. It looks violent. Artificial. Like a color that shouldn't exist without consequence.

FOR HUMAN CONSUMPTION—is labeled on the front.

What kind of mad scientist left this behind?

Carefully, I try to set it back down, but it slips out of my grasp.

The vial shatters on the ground.

Liquid spreads across the floor in careful spirals, changing color as it moves—

purple shifting to silver, silver turning mirror-smooth.

Reflected in the surface—it's me back in the mirror room.

I watch myself reach into the glass.

But this time, a different hand appears, it rises from the liquid in front of me.

Silver.

Slender.

Dripping.

Reaching for my face.

I fall backward, scrambling on the floor—hands slipping as I try to get away.

Cold fingers wrap around my ankle.

I kick.

I scream.

It won't let go.

The hand stretches itself up out of the puddle on the floor—a forearm, an elbow, a shoulder—gripping me tighter, dragging itself into existence.

My breath is ragged.

My chest hurts.

I fight like hell to claw my way to safety, but nothing I do shakes it off of me.

Briefly, I glimpse at the image on the floor—my hand pulling back from the mirror—breaking the connection.

The silver apparition in front of me lets go—melts.

It folds inward—losing form—sinking back into itself.

The surface of the liquid dulls and fades back into a dark purple. Then it begins to dry.

In seconds, it crusts over into a black stain on the floor.

I push myself up, clumsy, and stumble out of the room.

***

Danger is soaking every inch of this place. I can feel it oozing all around me.

I have to get out of here. Now.

Panic helps me forget why I left Room 107, and I go back to grab my keys and bag.

The door is still open.

But the mirror is gone.

I don't know what's real anymore.

Carelessly slinging my backpack over my shoulder, I hurry to leave.

Room 107 slams the door shut in my face.

The lock clicks.

No no no no—just no.

Nothing I do opens the door.

Fuck this madhouse. I'll crawl out of the window if I have to.

Was that window even here before?

I approach carefully.

The parking lot is dark, but there's enough light from the motel sign to see my car—

not too far from the window.

I unlatch it and slowly push it open.

Sunlight pours in through the gap—soft at first, then brighter.

What the hell?

A breeze follows.

The higher I raise the pane, the more I see.

A neighborhood.

Quiet. Suburban. Ordinary.

Cars passing.

Children on bikes.

Voices. Laughter.

The kind of day no one ever remembers because nothing happened.

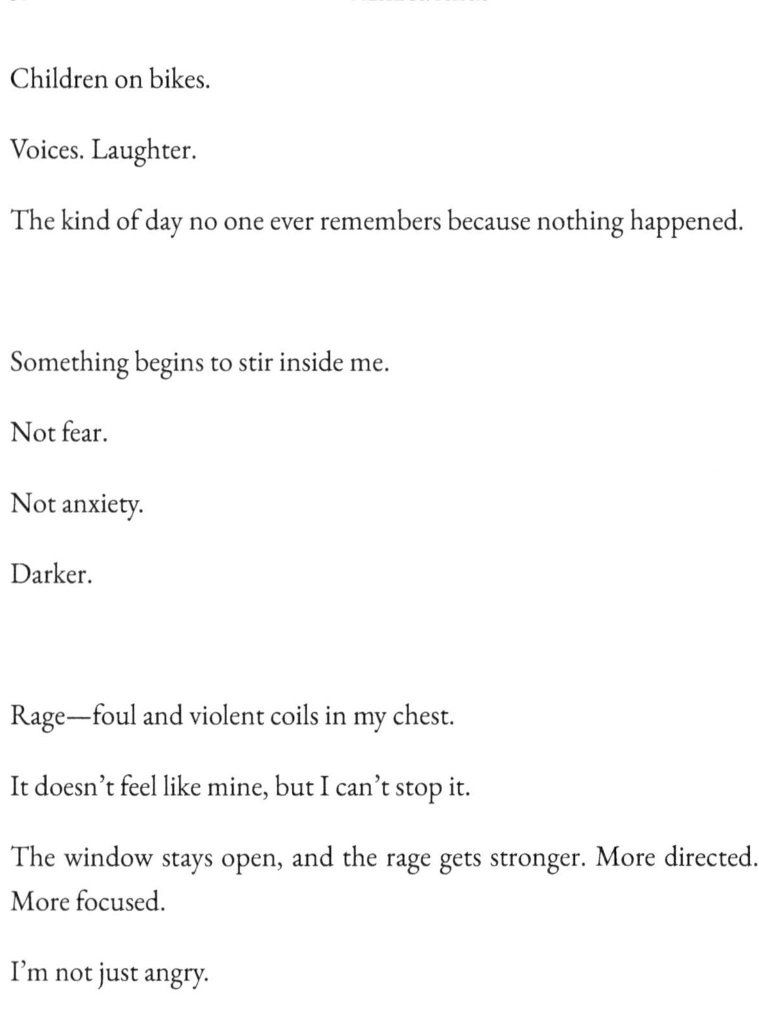

Something begins to stir inside me.

Not fear.

Not anxiety.

Darker.

Rage—foul and violent coils in my chest.

It doesn't feel like mine, but I can't stop it.

The window stays open, and the rage gets stronger. More directed. More focused.

I'm not just angry.

I'm burning from the inside with hatred.

Hatred for those that saw and looked away.

Hatred for the pretense of that perfect little neighborhood.

Hatred for myself.

Acid fills my lungs as I try to breathe, and I struggle against the madness that threatens to consume me.

I slam the window shut with both hands.

The lock clicks.

The feelings vanish.

***

The air feels thick. Heavy.

I turn slowly from the window and face the room. And stop.

My heart is pounding before I even understand why.

In the middle of the room now is a small, stained mattress.

It's dirty. Filthy.

I can smell the remnants of human waste and fear.

Something happened here.

I don't want to know what.

I close my eyes and find myself again—save myself again.

The door slowly creaks open.

I don't breathe.

I don't think.

I flee.

THE IN-BETWEEN

The train slows and stops between stations. No announcement. No flicker of light. Just stillness.

I glance around the empty car. I'm alone.

Or I was.

There's someone sitting across from me now.

Rain patters on the roof above us while the stranger sits perfectly still—legs crossed, arms folded, eyes hidden behind round black sunglasses.

Who the hell wears sunglasses on a train? At night?

As if in response, he reaches up, removes his glasses slowly, and slides them into his jacket pocket. His gaze never leaves mine.

The train hums beneath my feet, but it isn't moving. Outside, there is only mist. No city. No tracks. Just fog pressing against the windows like the world has stopped existing.

He adjusts his coat and taps two fingers on the seat beside him. When he lifts his hand, a small black envelope is sitting there.

"I wasn't sure you'd ever come back," he says quietly, handing the envelope to me.

Why does weird shit like this always happen to me?

Last week, my neighbor swore I'd stolen her goldfish while it was actively swimming in the tank behind her.

The stranger grins then, like he's in on some cosmic joke.

I swear, if he accuses me of stealing his hamster or newspaper, I'm going to lose it.

He laughs suddenly—deep, musical, and unsettling.

What the hell is funny?

I take the envelope from him, and he says—still laughing— "I knew I'd like you."

I narrow my eyes. "I'm not here to make friends."

He leans back like I've just offered him champagne. "Even better."

I look down at the envelope. It feels heavier than paper should. Thick, matte black. There's no seal. No return address.

I hesitate, then open it.

A single object slips into my palm.

I turn the coin over.

On one side—my face. Not metaphorically. My actual face.

On the other, engraved in small, precise lettering:

Flip to choose.
Heads: Return.
Tails: Remember.

"What is this?" I ask, looking up.

The seat across from me is now empty again.

He's gone.

***

The red emergency glow fades as the overhead lights flicker back on.

Had they even gone out?

I look at the coin still in my hand. Raise it to my mouth on instinct—like some old-timey prospector checking for real gold—then pause.

Yeah. Let's lick the mystery coin. That's smart.

I turn it again in my hand.

Return... to where? Remember... what?

I shrug. "Screw it."

I toss the coin into the air. Each turn catches the light, flashing between my face and the words.

I lift my hand to catch it—

Before it lands, a hand closes gently around it.

When did he come back?

"Tails," he says, palm open showing the result. Then meets my eyes. "Remember." And places the coin in my hand.

***

The world tilts— a dream slipping sideways.

The lights above us flicker once. In the blink between seconds, they become gas lamps.

The sterile walls melt into dark wood and gold trim. Outside the windows, a countryside rolls past—sepia-toned and unreal.

My breath catches in my throat.

I stumble back into my seat, gripping the coin like an anchor.

He doesn't move. Just watches me.

Then—

A voice.

My voice.

Small. Frantic. Echoing in a way that makes my stomach lurch.

"Please don't forget me."

There, reflected in the window, is a child.

A girl. Eight, maybe nine. Tears streak her face. Her eyes are wide, frantic. Terrified.

She looks exactly like me.

The train surges forward—this time too fast. The countryside outside blurs, warps, bends like wet paint sliding off canvas.

My vision doubles.

I grip the armrest with one hand, the coin with the other, like either of them might keep me from slipping into whatever this is.

The child is still watching me.

"Do you remember now?" she asks.

Something cracks in me. Not loud. Not sharp. Just a deep, quiet splintering.

I shake my head.

Grief that burns like fire fills my chest, consuming the oxygen from my lungs.

I squeeze my eyes shut.

Voices flood in—echoes layered over each other. Some are mine. Some aren't. Some speak in languages I don't recognize but understand. They chant, whisper, plead. Each one screaming through every layer of my being.

My body can't hold all of it. I fall forward onto my knees, gasping.

The coin burns in my hand now. I try to drop it, but my fingers won't open. It wants me to remember. It's forcing me.

A sob breaks loose from my throat—sharp and primal. It doesn't sound like it belongs to this world.

The walls collapse outward, dissolving into the night.

Nothing remains, but me—and him.

***

Slowly, he takes a step towards me.

"You weren't supposed to come back this way," he says, voice low, breaking with sorrow.

I look up at him through blurred vision. My throat is raw.

"What happened to me?" I whisper.

"You remembered too much before you were ready."

He kneels down beside me.

"You always were impatient," he says softly. "Even when you were divine."

I stare at him, hands trembling—gripping my head as I try to keep the shattered pieces of myself together.

The air feels too thin. My body isn't mine—it's too full, too loud.

"You were never supposed to remember like this," he says quietly.

"What is this?" I manage to whisper. "What did you do to me?"

"You asked to forget," he says. "And I helped you."

"Forget what?"

He hesitates.

"Your name."

That stops me cold.

"My... what?"

He steps closer—not threatening, just present. Heavy with something I don't understand yet.

"The name that holds who you really are," he says. "The one the world couldn't hold. You gave it up in the bargain."

Something shifts in the air between us.

"I've kept it safe," he adds. "Like you asked."

His hand unfolds to reveal a flame.

Small and powerful—I can hear its song.

The flame moves toward me in recognition.

I stare at it, transfixed.

It touches me before I touch it—wraps itself around me like it was waiting for this moment, and sinks beneath my skin, returning to where it belongs.

My knees hit the ground.

Sorrow.

Longing.

Grief.

I close my eyes and let it all in.

The air turns hot, swirling around me.

I feel like I'm being dragged under.

The world shifts.

The ground sinks.

***

Standing in my kingdom, I now know what was lost.

I remember who I am, who I was, and who I became.

I remember it all.

And my name.

Persephone.

PHASE THREE: POSSESSION

The body is not safe.
The soul is not alone.
The thing that's becoming you doesn't ask permission.

Fear

Fear has an inky black hole in the

center of its space.

Its gravity pulls and distorts

logic and reason.

It's surrounded by cloudy yellow specks of regret

barely visible

around the event horizon.

GROCERY RUN

Rows of fluorescent lights above me blink off one by one. The freezer section goes quiet mid hum.

Of course.

My cart squeaks to a stop in the middle of the aisle.

My brain's already spiraling.

Don't they have backup generators in these places? They make enough money to afford one.

Other shoppers mumble and shuffle around on adjacent aisles, making lame jokes about "being in the dark."

I just want to finish shopping and go home.

I fumble for my phone.

Light.

Something....

CRACK. CRACK. CRACK.

The air changes.

People are screaming.

Terror—thick, alive—fills the voices rising from the aisles.

My face goes cold.

I can feel my heartbeat in my teeth.

Screaming.

Rushing.

It's everywhere.

CRACK CRACK CRACK CRACK

Oh god.

No no no no—

I can't see.

Shit.

My legs shake beneath me.

This can't be happening.

More screaming.

High-pitched. Close.

A shelf breaks—tin cans and plastic bottles crash to the tile floor—it sounds like a dam breaking.

Danger is surrounding me—

wrapping around my ankles, folding my feet into the concrete.

A woman pleads for mercy—

She's on the aisle right next to me.

Oh god.

I don't know where I'm going—

just that I have to get out.

Survive.

Eggs and milk long forgotten—

I run.

A corner, barely visible with the help of my phone.

I feel the edge with my hands.

Sharp. Cold.

The chaos around me dies down.

Silence.

Only soft sobs now.

I scan ahead—

there.

The exit.

Safety.

Freedom.

I can make it.

I can—

A decision snaps inside me.

I go for it.

I take one step—

It comes from nowhere.

Too real.

Too fast.

—and a sweaty hand grabs my arm.

Cold metal presses against my temple.

CLICK

Domestic Bliss

The evening sun casts a golden haze across the living room, softening the edges of everything it touches.

I'm tired.

The kind of tired that sinks deep, that makes the couch feel like it's pulling me under. The light is warm against my skin—soft and quiet, like it's coaxing me to surrender. My eyes start to close.

I'm fully melted into the couch, half-asleep, when I hear it.

A soft rustling sound.

Too soft to place, but close.

Too close.

My eyes snap open.

I hold still. Listen.

There it is again.

Definitely coming from under the couch.

Immediately, my brain offers its favorite disaster scenario:

Snake.

Because obviously it's a snake. That's always where my head goes—straight to nightmare fuel.

I lie there another second, hoping I imagined it.

A faint vibration begins thumping against the underside of the couch—

like something shifting. Moving. Waiting.

I bolt upright, and leap a full step away, just in case whatever it is wants to launch itself at my ankles.

What the actual hell?

It's like my life is a long-running joke, and today my peaceful nap is the punchline.

I try to shake it off. Give myself a little pep talk.

Okay. Deep breath. There's probably a reasonable explanation.

Don't panic. Just peek under the couch.

If it's nothing, I go back to napping.

If it's a snake... well, I'll die of a stroke before it even gets the chance to bite me.

I close my eyes, grab the arm of the couch, and pull it hard—launching it into the middle of the room.

For a second, I can't open my eyes. I don't want to see what's waiting for me.

I squint one eye open.

No snake.

Thank the gods.

But, my relief and unexpected religious conversion is short-lived.

Pushed up through the cracked floorboards is a small, tangled cluster of roots and vines.

Dark. Wet-looking.

And definitely not supposed to be here.

I lean in without meaning to.

There's something about the way the sprigs catch the light—

a soft, iridescent glow that pulses and fades, like breath trying to remember its rhythm.

It's strange.

Lovely, almost.

I keep watching. Mesmerized.

The shimmer.

The movement.

The slow, steady twitch of something alive.

It's so beau—

Before I know it, my hand is already reaching out.

Fingers brushing the surface like I was always going to touch it.

Like I didn't have a choice.

It slithers around my hand.

Oh shit.

I panic and try to pull away, but it only tightens—like it's desperately holding on.

My brow is sweating. The pain is excruciating—radiating up my arm, setting fire to every nerve ending.

My vision tunnels. I'm going to pass out.

My knees hit the floor.

The root is sliding up my wrist now—quick, certain.

It knows exactly what it's doing.

I try to scream, but it catches in my throat.

My hand...

I watch in horror as my skin starts to disappear. As if this plant is drinking me whole and leaving itself in my place.

My arm now ends in something that shouldn't belong to me—

wooden, roped, pulsing like it remembers being alive.

Something inside me is pulling away from the surface.

I collapse onto the floor and watch helplessly as inch by inch, my body becomes unrecognizable as human. Layers upon twisted layers of roots and vines replace and transform the shape of me.

I can't move.

I can't scream.

Imprisoned behind a wall of thorns.

What am I?

Why is this happening to me?

My screams are trapped in silence, as a dark silhouette rises from the cracked floorboards.

She steps out into the light.

Fully formed.

Wearing my skin.

She wipes the dust from her palms and smiles.

Not cruel.

Not kind.

Just... satisfied.

Standing over me, she says nothing—looking at me lying there.

In silence, I thrash against the bars holding my mind captive.

I cry.

I scream.

I beg.

PLEASE LET ME OUT. My life isn't supposed to end this way...

Fury blurs into exhaustion.

It's hopeless. This is how I end...

My head lolls to the side—tears slide down my face as I feel the last of myself start to fade.

Delight flickers in her soulless eyes.

Then she steps over my body—

and walks away.

Lawn People

Whoever invented SNOOZE should win a version of the Nobel Peace Prize that rewards diabolical genius.

After losing my battle with the alarm clock, I zombie-walk into the kitchen.

Caffeine. I need it.

The coffee machine groans to life and starts filling my mug. The smell alone is enough to reassemble my soul.

I take a sip, shuffle toward the window, and stop mid-slurp.

There's a crowd of strangers standing on my lawn.

Just... standing there. Not moving. Not speaking.

One of them holds a sign:

Don't be alarmed. We're just waiting.

What the actual fuck?

Muttering obscenities to myself, I throw on shoes and go outside.

I don't need this today. It's like I have a beacon that attracts weird.

I just broke up with a guy who thought ghost hunting was a viable retirement plan—now there's a full cult meeting on my lawn.

***

Outside, I take a step closer and briefly consider spraying them with the hose.

Every head turns in unison.

All eyes on me.

Ho-ly shit.

"Alright, this has been fun and all," I start, inching toward unhinged, "but—"

I stop.

They all shift their heads upward. Slowly. Together.

"Hey," I stammer, "can you all go do your weird... whatever this is... somewhere else?"

Nothing.

No response.

Just eyes locked on the sky.

"HELLO?" I wave like I'm flagging down a taxi from the void.

Still nothing.

My mother always said curiosity would get me in trouble someday.

Against my better judgment, I look up. I'd hate to prove her wrong.

So, we stand there.

Looking up.

Saying nothing.

What am I doing?

I feel as insane as they are.

That's it. I'm getting the hose. I've tried being reasonable, but clearly these people don't understand the danger of interrupting my morning coffee routine.

I turn toward the garden shed—

—and one of them is suddenly in front of me.

No sound. No footsteps.

Just... there.

Eyes distant. Unblinking.

"No. It's not time yet."

You've got to be kidding me.

"My lawn is not a sacred gathering place for your little 'club,'" I say, air-quoting with aggressive fingers.

"Leave. Now."

"Soon," they all say together.

One of them—a woman in a polka-dotted raincoat—steps forward, moving with slow, robotic grace.

Her voice doesn't match her face.

Too deep. Too many voices layered at once.

"We're here for the convergence."

I blink. "You're here for the what?"

She points at the patch of overgrown grass by the mailbox.

"This is the last known location."

I glance down.

There's nothing there but a rock, a plastic fork, and a patch of clover.

"...Of what?" I ask, because apparently I hate peace.

She doesn't answer.

None of them do.

Suddenly, one guy pulls out a chair from nowhere and sits down.

Then another pulls out a cooler.

Someone starts passing out sandwiches.

A kid in the back produces a kazoo from his sleeve and just... starts playing.

"I'm going to lose my mind," I whisper.

I hope they have beer in that cooler. I'm going to need it.

Just as I decide now is the perfect time to scream, throw something, or both—

a sound rumbles overhead.

Not quite thunder.

Something lower.

Older.

Every head tilts—exactly twelve degrees to the left.

In perfect sync.

They point.

At me.

"You're early," they say in unison.

"You're tres-pass-ing," I snap back, slow and mocking.

The kazoo makes a sad, broken squeak.

Early? These people don't know me at all. I've never been early to anything in my life.

They begin to put away their sandwiches and party favors.

The cooler vanishes.

The chairs are gone.

They look back to the sky.

Then one voice:

"Do you see?"

Another:

"Do you see?"

Louder now:

"Do you see?"

It becomes a chant.

A chorus.

"Do you see? Do you see? Do you see?"

***

The sky cracks open.

The world goes black.

The kazoo? It keeps playing.

PHASE FOUR:
Threshold

Reality doesn't crack here—it invites you to shift.

You're not leaving the way you entered.

Asymmetry

His whiskers felt too deliberate, too symmetrical—like they'd been chosen.

He sat beneath the old oak tree, tail twitching in the dirt, but he wasn't fooled.

It wasn't a tree.

He wasn't a cat.

And something was waiting for him to remember why either of those lies had been told.

Every time the wind rustled the leaves above him, he was more certain:

the tree was watching him back.

The cat sat unmoving for a while.

Can cats have existential crises? he wondered.

It must be so—because that's what he was having.

When he rubbed against the tree, he sensed something.

Did the tree know more than it was saying?

Was it friend or foe?

He decided it didn't matter. He was here now, and so was the tree.

He stretched in the grass and felt the cold dew on his fur.

A single leaf rustled loose, twirling and dancing through the air toward his face—

a little green friend saying hello.

VENDING MACHINE

Late afternoon light peeks through the leaves of the forest, as I stare in wonder at a vending machine nestled in a patch of moss between the trees.

The glass is dusty, the buttons worn down.

Inside—a single book sits alone untouched by time.

My breath catches.

I recognize the engraved symbol on the cover.

This book is ancient. It hasn't revealed itself for at least a century.

I've heard the legends. It only appears when you need it most. Only to those it chooses. The book is said to give you an answer you didn't know you needed.

But there's always a price.

I walk around to the side, searching for a mechanism.

A digital display glows to life, scrolling a single line:

PAY THE PRICE. TELL ME YOUR TRUTH.

My truth?

How do I know my truth?

I watch the display again, wishing the price was something I had to give.

I sit down beside the machine, despair and melancholy competing for my attention.

I know if my answer isn't true—

even if I don't realize it—

the book will disappear.

Lost to me forever.

I close my eyes.

Breathe.

Why is this so hard?

The truth is in me. I can feel it. But words are a poor translator for something that feels like a knowing wrapped in fog.

I stand again.

Peer through the glass.

The book is still there.

Waiting.

Beautiful.

Unreachable—unless I'm honest.

I'm afraid.

Afraid the right words won't find their way out.

That even my subconscious will betray me.

"I can't," I whisper.

"I'm sorry."

Tears I didn't expect blur my vision as I turn to walk away.

But behind me—

a whirring sound.

Mechanical.

Alive.

I spin back around just in time to see the vending machine vanish.

In its place,

resting gently on the forest floor—

the book.

THE HOUSE

Mornings here are the hardest. I always wake expecting my home, my bed, my life... but I'm always disappointed.

The walls curve gently into my silences.

The rooms shift like emotions I can't bring myself to name.

My room looks familiar, but it's not the same as mine.

How long have I been here?

When did I walk inside?

How did it take shape?

Each day I spend here, I ask the same questions—but there are no answers.

The house wraps itself around me like it's always been, but I can't tell if it's protecting me or keeping me from leaving.

***

Most days here are the same.

Nothing remarkable.

Just me and a house I don't remember building.

Some mornings, the windows are bricked shut with memories.

Other days, they swing open on their own—letting light spill across the floor like forgiveness when I'm spiraling in shame for things I still can't face.

At first, I liked it here. The rooms felt like purpose. The quiet felt like an oasis.

But now—

I don't want to be here anymore.

I've walked through every room. I've searched every corner. Still no answers. No exits. But I keep searching anyway.

***

Today, something changes.

I find a door I've never seen before.

The wood is darker than the rest of the house—its grain deep and weathered, its hinges worn to the edge of rust.

It doesn't match the house.

It's too old.

Too still.

Too anchored.

I reach for the knob and try to turn it.

Locked.

I jiggle it, press against it, lean in harder—still nothing. My hand lingers on the metal, warm from touch, and that's when I notice the keyhole beneath the handle.

I kneel, lean forward, and look through.

There's nothing on the other side.

Just darkness.

A frustrated exhale leaves me, and I think about walking away, but something stops me—

a soft rustling sound, like leaves falling in autumn.

A worn piece of parchment slides out from beneath the door and stops at my feet.

Across the page, scrawled in dark ink:

"don't give up so quick."

***

Back in my room, I sit with the note and read it again.

After all this time, the house is finally speaking to me.

I don't know how I know it's meant for me, but I do. I cradle it like something precious—a gift.

Color begins to seep through the walls—shimmering blues textured with something delicate and suspended—like crushed crystal, weightless in the air.

Hope.

I'm still holding the parchment when the ink begins to swirl, sinking and reappearing—until it reshapes itself into a crudely drawn map.

My first instinct is suspicion.

It always is.

But I push it down.

Trust is a decision I make in that moment.

Whatever happens next is on my terms, in this house.

***

The map leads me down a hallway I've walked a hundred times—only now, it feels longer.

Photos I've never seen before begin to appear, one by one, lining the walls.

I look at them all.

Memories of me that aren't mine.

In one, I'm a child—smiling, with a family I don't recognize.

In another, I'm on a beach with people I've never met.

Parties. Weddings. Vacations. Quiet moments.

She's living a life I never lived.

Near the end, a photo of me—older, laughing, radiant.

Her smile looks like it used to belong to me. I wish I knew her. I think we could have been friends.

An ache I'm not ready for cuts through my reverie and reminds me to keep going.

***

The hallway ends at an empty room with no door. Just an open frame, like an invitation—so I take it, and step inside.

The second I do, a soft breeze lifts my hair—like the room just exhaled, and a strange current skips across my skin.

I turn around—but the doorway is gone.

An empty room just moments ago, is now lined with bookshelves that stretch from floor to ceiling.

The house has never been this alive before.

Candlelight flickers across heavy Victorian furniture—like I've stepped into a library from another century.

My breath catches.

There it is again—the old wooden door.

***

Footsteps echo from the hallway.

Then voices.

Laughter.

Faint at first, but getting closer.

Odd. I've always been alone here...

As the doorknob turns, I look for a place to hide and duck beneath a large writing desk.

Three men enter the room.

Two of them look... familiar.

But I can't place how or why.

The third is a stranger.

From my hiding place, I watch him with curiosity.

He moves with quiet confidence, settles into a reading chair, and starts thumbing through a book, smiling faintly to himself.

He's beautiful in a way that has nothing to do with vanity.

I slowly try to adjust myself without making any noise—it's so cramped under here.

Oh, this is ridiculous. Why am I the one hiding?

I'm not the intruder.

I unfold myself and clumsily rise to my feet.

The man with the book startles when he sees me.

The book slips from his lap and lands on the floor with a dull thud.

The other two men turn toward the sound.

That's when I notice what they're wearing—tailored suits, ruffled collars, candlelight flickering across their sleeves.

"Bloody hell, Seb, take it easy on the whisky," the blond man laughs.

Seb doesn't laugh.

The other two shake their heads in joking exasperation and turn back to their conversation.

Only Seb is watching me.

He stands slowly, eyes never leaving mine.

"How did you get here?" he asks, voice low—measured, like he doesn't want to scare me off.

I glance toward the other two, still deep in conversation.

He follows my gaze, then leans in slightly.

"Don't worry about them," he says, softer now. "They can't see you."

I blink. "What do you mean they can't see me?"

He smiles faintly, almost apologetically.

"They're part of the house."

What does that even mean?

I open my mouth. Close it. Try again.

"Well, I just... woke up here. The house felt familiar. But I don't remember walking in."

I tell him about the shifting rooms.

The door.

The message.

The map...

His eyes widen. I stop.

"...How did you get here?"

He looks at me with fascination.

"I always come here when I want to be alone."

I glance at the two men still laughing behind him.

"...Doesn't look very alone."

He grins. "You never miss anything, do you?"

My pulse quickens at the way he says it, but I try to ignore it.

He walks back to his chair and sinks into it with a sigh, running a hand through his hair.

His eyes go distant, like he's talking to himself now.

"I never expected anyone else to be here."

"Where is here?"

He considers the question for a long moment.

"This is where I come when I'm searching for answers."

He glances around the room. "It's different every time. But always familiar."

He pauses. "I think the house builds itself from memory."

I tilt my head. "Yours?"

A small smile plays at the edge of his mouth. "Sometimes."

He reaches down to retrieve the book he dropped earlier.

Holds it without opening it.

Like it means something.

"I used to think this was a place made for me," he says—looking at me in a way that says more than his words.

"Now I'm not so sure."

The fire crackles in the silence between us.

Somewhere in the distance, a clock ticks—but I can't see one.

"Is this your memory, then?" I ask.

He finally looks up again.

"I don't know. Maybe it's ours."

I don't respond—his words feel true like this isn't the first time I've heard him say it.

He nods toward a silver box sitting on the table next to him.

"I think this belongs to you. It's never appeared here before."

He watches me. Quiet. Waiting.

I reach over and take the box.

A key rests on a delicate velvety pillow inside.

A hum—barely audible—fills the room as I take the key in my hand.

"...What happens if I use it?"

My voice sounds strange—further away than it should be.

He studies me for a long moment.

"I don't know," he says. "But you came all this way."

I glance down at the key in my hand.

My pulse won't slow.

"I should probably... get back. To... um... my home."

He doesn't laugh at me.

Just watches.

Like he hears what I'm not saying.

I take a breath and try to recover.

"This whole thing is just... weird."

His smile softens. "Yeah. It is."

I turn the key over in my hand.

It's heavier than it looks.

Warmer, too.

He doesn't try to stop me.

Doesn't tell me what I should do.

He just says,

"Whatever happens… you won't be lost."

My throat tightens at the words.

I step toward the door.

The world tilts.

A sharp sound—like wind and thunder all at once—rattles the walls.

Then stillness.

The room is empty.

But the door is open.

PHASE FIVE:
INTEGRATION

You arrive—

not where you were,

but where you are.

Connection

Iridescent blues and soft grays intertwine.

Neuronal currents branch in every direction.

They light up in recognition of safety.

Gold sparks gently fly out like a flare

when they find connection.

GOLDEN THREAD

My emotions float around me in visible threads. All unique in texture and color—beautiful and delicate.

Sometimes I wonder why I'm the only one who experiences emotions this way. Do other people know that joy—so bold and vibrant on its own—often weaves itself with the strands of pain—dulling it? Making it harder to see. Harder to feel.

The threads never leave me. They braid—connect and bind with each other, creating intricate patterns.

I see it all.

I feel it all.

Loneliness hovers around me now, creating tight webs around the others.

Just when I thought I'd accepted its presence as a permanent fixture around me—

A thread unlike any other I've seen, golden and glowing, breaks through the shadows and highlights a path before me. The other threads go opaque in its shine.

I feel the thread tugging at me—and that tug feels familiar, but it's not a thread of mine.

I wrap my index finger around the slack that hangs above me and gently pull.

It glows brighter.

Excitement and curiosity are weaving around me.

I trace my fingers along the thread, not fearing where the path leads.

I find myself near the mouth of a cave.

It's so dark I can't see anything, but the longer I walk, the brighter it glows.

Even though I'm afraid, I follow the thread into the darkness.

As I walk deeper in, the golden thread begins to spark. Flecks of gold dance around in the air.

I notice a light up ahead—

standing in the opening is the silhouette of a man.

"Where have you been? I've been waiting for you," he says.

Softly, he continues, "I tied this thread to you so you could find me when you were ready."

I walk closer to him and look up into his face.

His smile is familiar.

He laughs, and I know that laugh.

I think I should be afraid, but I've never felt safer.

I ask, "Who are you?"

He reaches out and gently strokes my cheek with his thumb.

It feels like he's touched me this way a thousand times before.

I close my eyes—

and suddenly his hand is gone.

When I open them again, he's looking at me with both longing and pain so strong it almost feels like my own.

The golden thread is dancing between us. It pulses with something I don't have a name for—but I understand it.

He says, "I'm here to take you home."

I hear the truth in his voice. The connection we share with our threads—we both see it. We both feel it.

At that instant, the golden thread glows blinding white and swirls between us.

The light is so bright I want to close my eyes—

but it's so beautiful I have to watch.

Each end of the thread starts to connect.

I look over, and he's watching me, but I can't take my eyes off the thread as it begins to take the shape of an opening.

The once-blinding light is now a portal—

and beyond, I can see a beautiful green field with rolling hills—it looks like home— and a worn dirt path that leads to the opening.

I can't help myself. I'm smiling.

He reaches out his hand and says,

"Are you ready?"

I don't look back.

I take his hand, and together, we step onto the dirt path.

Layers of Beauty

I didn't know my body had been bracing for so long until it finally stopped.

The spikes running along my edges retract and the static fades.

The room is quiet. Only breath and the evening light as witness.

The space in between my soul and skin settles.

There's no war to fight here.

Nothing to defend.

No chafing of my edges.

Just two currents playing together—electrical harmony.

My energy dances alongside his.

It's never met a friend before.

An unseen force pulses in the air around me.

Is this joy?

Is this love?

Does it even have a name?

I have so many questions, but no language to ask them.

It's safe to ache here.

To wonder here.

To feel here.

To be.

The guardian beneath my skin put away its claws and began to purr.

Eyes that burn with knowing stare into mine as gentle fingers trace the lines of my face.

This is what it feels like to be alive.

Elemental

The depths have always been its home—though it feels like it has just arrived.

It slipped beneath the surface. Sank into something familiar.

It moves—slow at first. A curious flick of the fin. A shift in weight.

Does it remember how to swim, or is it learning?

It glides, propelled by something it doesn't name. A feeling. A pull.

The mission is clear: find the source.

It doesn't know what the source is. It only knows it must.

Here in the deep, gravity forgets its rules. The world tilts into weightlessness.

It rolls and spins, letting cold seaweed drag across its belly like a ribbon.

Joy flickers.

It plays.

But something echoes.

A sound not of noise—but of instinct.

A summons.

It stills.

The joy was only borrowed.

The pull grows stronger.

The source is nearby.

Instincts older than thought take over.

The surface is close.

Fins cut faster through the dark, chasing light that ripples above like broken mirrors and forgotten time.

Currents cradle it. Push it forward.

It does not falter.

The source is calling.

With strength and precision, it breaks the surface—

flying, soaring, basking in the sun for a moment.

Only a moment.

The sacred source is meant to be felt—

even for those who do not live in its presence.

The orca dives back down into the silent depths.

Vanishing beneath the waves.

Until next time.

CLOSING

You came apart.

And you arrived in pieces,

but still glowing.

This is not the end of you.

When Words Aren't Enough

Scan below using your Spotify app for the music that inspired the madness.

[Fragments of Cerulean—Spotify playlist by MeowDragon]

You made it to the end!

For more information on Fragments of Cerulean, future projects, or to stay connected:

Here's where to find me:

@revelationhouse.works

Thank you for reading.